The Leaf That Never Fell .... p. 3

The Chef Who Lost His Salsa .... p. 20

Stop 36 .... p. 33

Punk Is Not Dead .... p. 41

Lolita's Chatty Casa .... p. 52

illustrated by
Maddison Kitching

THE LEAF THAT NEVER FELL

The Leaf That Never Fell

Tony lived on possibly the most charming street in Melbourne: Carlton-bound, with park lining one side and triple-brick Victorian castles on the other. And each morning, he was blessed with the glorious orange sun waking him as it bounced through the shadows and off the luscious, healthy green grass. Others regularly told Tony that he was absolutely living the dream. These others were the hundreds of leaves just like Tony, living on the heritage-listed oak tree. But, nothing that good can last forever, right?

'At some point, at some stage, reality comes knocking,' his fellow leaves would tell him. 'You know well and good Tony that, come autumn, we will all fall and blow into the real world, into humans, and into our destined lives—that's what is really waiting for us,' they would often remind him. 'Stop getting too attached.'

'No no no,' Tony would respond. 'What you fail to appreciate is this moment exactly. This is life's purpose, what it's all about—you know?'

The other leaves never took Tony seriously because Tony was far older than them. In fact, he had twenty years on the entire stump because each autumn Tony never fell off the tree. He was the only leaf in the entire city that was yet to touch the ground. There were rumours of another one on the coast, a leaf so strong, thick and stubborn that not even the ocean's blistering breeze could push him off. Aside from this leaf, Tony was the only one of his kind, and he wished to stay that way. He didn't believe in the next best thing, or that destiny was even real; he had his life on the old oak tree, and that was perfect. No myth or strong wind could change that. And so he sat and sat and held on tight with all of his might, weathering each wind, storm and blow. Tony sat on the old oak tree as a happy, simple leaf. Each spring, around mid-September, after he had spent the entire winter alone on the tree, Tony would spot the first sprout. Excited about the new friends he would make, Tony would watch the new leaves slowly grow. He would keep his soon-to-be friends encouraged by reading them poetry—his own poetry, of course, about life on the tree and the lifelong friends he met along the way: Frank, Vivina and his best friend, Carlos, who had held on tight all autumn to spend every moment with Tony. They would sit and play poker with chips made of beer caps and cards made of bark that the birds, as they swung by, would drop to the two. Carlos was the last leaf to fall that season, taken by a sudden gust of wind. As Carlos blew away, Tony noticed his frightened expression, which quickly broke into one of joy as he thought about his new-found freedom ahead. Tony thought, in this one rare moment, about going with him, but in what seemed like the same moment, he turned to writing poetry—his regular release.

Carlos goodbye
Not sad
Not I
The greatest player
The tree set eye
We sat
We were
We never spoke
Of life beyond
The heritage oak
But you, you see
Not words you need
To nearly take me off this tree
I saw your tight
I saw your fright
I saw you joy into the night
Carlos, the great player
Perhaps now life as a Casino Major
Until we sit again—Tony

The Leaf That Never Fell

Tony had met plenty of leaves on the oak in his time, but it was hard watching Carlos blow away, and Tony continually felt a missing presence after he left. Tony kept a look out for people with cards passing by, thinking Carlos was coming to say hello, but, truth be told, he didn't know if, after they flew away, the leaves remembered their lives as leaves at all. He only hoped that one day a kind, calm man would look up and say, 'Bet you can't beat me today.'

But such thoughts only harmed Tony. He had to think that life was better on the tree, with his Carlton Gardens sun that no life on the ground could offer. And so he opened his journal and read his recent poems to the sprouts and soon-to-be-new friends:

> *Life on a tree*
> *Is splendid you see*
> *The Melbourne Museum*
> *Gifts all kinds to see*
> *From here you can view*
> *A dinosaur's shoe*
> *And IMAX projects*
> *Nothing short of huge*
> *And when the leaves shed*
> *It at times hurts my head*
> *I smile with excitement*
> *Of my new friends ahead— Tony*

After finishing his poem, he closed his book and decided to have a nap. After all, he was the only leaf on the tree, and the sun had just set. And so he napped—a long, peaceful nap—as he did every year when there were no leaves chatting about. When he eventually peeled open his old, worn eyes, he looked closely at the identical oak opposite his. For the first time, he noticed the tree was not as bare as usual, spotting a single leaf that also had not fallen this season.

'Beautiful morning always this time of year isn't it?' the unknown leaf yelled over the park's path.

'One of the most peaceful ones, yes,' Tony responded. 'Sorry, I have never noticed you before. Did you hold on just this one season?' asked Tony, confused.

'Actually, no, I've been on this tree for nearly fifteen years. I just hide well behind the shade of the branches—I don't like the sun all that much,' the unknown leaf responded.

'That's not possible! The bounce of the sun that wakes me each rise is the reason I'm so tragically stuck on this beautiful tree,' Tony responded.

They both laughed and acknowledged the enjoyable conversation and each other's presence, which was incredibly rare for both leaves.

'Are you a poet?' the unknown leaf asked.

'Yes, I am. And what are you and who are you kind soul?' Tony asked.

'I'm Geraldine, and I'm not anyone. I don't do anything except sit here and watch the joy that encompasses this park: the picnics on Sundays, the girls that walk to work together and even the couples that come here to break up. As they walk off separately, they always seem the most joyous. These are rare moments.'

'It's nice to meet you, Geraldine. I'm Tony, and I'd love to hear more about the beautiful things that you have seen in our home. For so long, I've been concentrating on the leaves on my own tree that my eyes sometimes forget about what happens around it.'

'I'd love to, I mean, we have quite some time until we're overpopulated again. I'm certain each year more and more leaves grow, don't you think?' Geraldine proclaimed.

'My thoughts exactly!' Tony agreed.

'And how about those roadworks across the gardens. This used to be such a peaceful place before those loud bangs and crashes,' Geraldine went on.

'Tell me about it,' Tony responded with a gentle smirk.

They both smiled, a smile of undemanding compassion, and, for once, accompaniment. It seemed Tony's time on the tree was finally starting to come to some serious thought. Since Carlos's departure, Tony would be lying to himself if he said he didn't wonder each day where Carlos was and what he was doing. But, just like every other outlandish thought that crept into Tony's mind, this one inspired Tony to turn to poetry. But this time, he had a new inspiration—the wonderful Geraldine:

> *Carlos, I won't lie,*
> *Your departure asked me why*
> *Since you blew away*
> *There has not been a day*
> *Where I hadn't preferred*
> *You were here to stay*
>
> *But I met a new leaf*
> *Who has cleared up some grief*
> *Geraldine is her name,*
> *So, until I write again...–Tony*

'What are you writing there?' Geraldine shouted from the other side of the park.

'Oh, it's a new poem actually, ' Tony replied.

'Can I hear it?' Geraldine asked.

'If you'd like to, sure, wait one second,' Tony said. He rolled up his poem and held it in the air until a gust of wind was strong enough to blow it over to Geraldine. The wind swept the entire park, and Tony let go of the note, shouting, 'Here it is Geraldine, you better catch it!'

Geraldine laughed and purposefully got caught in the wind so she could stretch far enough to catch the poem. With excitement, she read it and felt equal parts happy and sad. 'So this Carlos, he means a lot to you, doesn't he?' Geraldine asked.

'Well, I guess you could say that, sure.'

'My love, Lucas, he lives just across the park there. I saw him blow off the tree and—BOOM—he was instantly a beautiful man living across the road. He even has the same rip in his shirt, just like he had as a leaf. Every Sunday, he comes and sits under my tree and drinks his coffee. When we were on the tree together, he promised he would come back. But he never speaks to me when he sits down, so I'm not sure if he remembers me at all or his life as a leaf. Either way, it's nice that he comes back. It's the highlight of my week.'

'I guess we'll never know unless we blow off the tree ourselves, Geraldine, but Carlos is not my love. We're just close friends, I'd say,' shared Tony.

'But you think about him and write about him? And you wish he was here? And you hope to see him again? Maybe live life together? Is that right?' Geraldine asked.

'Well, okay, I guess I do wish all of those things,' Tony agreed.

'And you've never wished this about any other leaf that you've met, is that right?'

'No, Geraldine, he is the only one, but I've never been in love before. I don't think this is love ... is it?' Tony asked.

'I can't answer that Tony, but I can tell just by this poem that Carlos means a lot to you,' Geraldine answered.

Tony said nothing, but felt as though something was starting to make sense for him. 'Do you write, Geraldine?' he asked her.

'Yes, actually, it's all I do on this tree. I write stories, and I read them to Lucas, but I'm not sure he can hear me, like I said.'

'Well, as we're about to brace for winter, and I've heard this winter is going to be stem-cold, why don't we write together? You write a story and blow it over here, and then I'll write a poem, and so on. I'm sure that will get us through the season,' Tony suggested.

'I'm in!' Geraldine proclaimed.

And so the two spent the entire winter writing poetry and stories and learning about each other's' lives: their deepest secrets, their regrets, their ambitions and more. Many of Tony's poems began to indicate that he wanted to leave the tree, and Geraldine wrote poetry back about how she never does. Together they wrote enough poems to make a large book, and, before they knew it, they'd reached the end of winter, and the new leaves were starting to form their shape. For once, Tony was not thrilled. Geraldine told Tony about a storm that was set to hit them the following week.

'We have to hold on tight this Wednesday, Tony. I've heard the winds are strong enough to blow our entire stumps over!' Ger-

The Leaf That Never Fell

aldine warned.

'Yes it's going to be a big one. Let's hold on at the same time and that way we can coach each other through it,' Tony suggested.

Geraldine accepted the offer, with a sad suspicion that Tony was setting up for their last encounter. On the day of the storm, winter had only a few days left, and the new leaves were growing with strength for the new season that was about to introduce itself. Tony was reading his poems to the new leaves, which seemed to give them extra strength and growth, while Geraldine was waiting for Lucas to come and visit her—it was Sunday.

Lucas arrived to visit Geraldine, or maybe he just came to drink his coffee as he does on the same seat every Sunday—she couldn't know for sure. Geraldine was sitting contently on the tree. Lucas finished his sip of coffee and turned around and looked up at the tree at Geraldine, which he had never done before.

'You really are a beautiful tree,' Lucas said before walking home. Geraldine was so happy that Tony could see her smile shining all the way from his tree. Suddenly, the weather started to grumble, rumble and turn, and Geraldine prepared for the storm.

'Why don't you just fly off Geraldine. You seem happy with Lucas,' Tony yelled through the increasing wind.

'What are you talking about, Tony? You know why—because life on the tree is where I want to be. There is no need for anything else. You know this Tony. You've been here longer than me!' Geraldine yelled. 'The storm is coming. We have to hold on and not chat!' she instructed.

The Leaf That Never Fell

Tony held onto the closest branch as the wind began to scream, and both Tony's and Geraldine's branches started to sway. 'But what if we need to stop resisting change and just fly with the wind? There's no saying that we can't enjoy the beauty of this tree and life as a human, just like Lucas.' Tony went on, as the wind started to shake his and Geraldine's bodies so viciously she could hardly respond.

'But ... there's no ... certainty ... that your destiny ... is better ... than this,' Geraldine yelled through the wind.

'But ... there's no certainty ... that it isn't,' Tony yelled loudly because he wasn't sure Geraldine could hear him over the sound of their bodies rattling in the wind.

It then started to rain and hail, making it even harder to hold on through the dramatic wind that had taken over Carlton Gardens.

'Make sure you come back Tony ... come back to visit me ... maybe on Wednesdays,' Geraldine shouted, as a parting gift to Tony, letting him know that she supported him.

Tony collected his last bit of energy and responded, 'I like Thursdays better at the park. Keep writing Geraldine.' He looked down at his stem, which was minutes away from breaking off, and, instead of holding on tighter, he finally let go, giving himself to the wind and to his destiny.

'WoooooooWWWwwwwwwWWWwwwwwWWWwwww' Tony screamed, as the wind whipped him in circles a thousand times over, and in what seemed like the next second, Tony was standing in front of a microphone, in front of a crowd of smiling people who were sitting and waiting for him to speak. The room was surrounded by books, and as Tony looked down at his hands, he noticed he was holding one himself titled *Poems of the Old Oak Tree* by Tony Frank. He instantly knew he was there to read one of his poems to the lovely group of people waiting to hear them.

'Oh, hello everyone. Thank you for coming today to hear my poetry. I'll read one of my favourites. It's called *Geraldine,*' Tony spoke softly into the microphone and cleared his throat.

    Winter this year
    Was warmer you see
   When usually I'm near frozen
    And stiff on the tree

    After everyone leaves
    A silence erupts
So I sit, and I write, and I wrap myself up

    Her name is Geraldine
    My dear friend
  She helped me know how to transcend
  Goodbye Geraldine and Old Oak Tree
I hope you're still there to sit with me—Tony

Tony finished his poem, and the crowd rose from their seats and clapped wholeheartedly. He thanked them profusely and even offered a bow, holding his book to his heart, already feeling like his destiny was something worth letting go for. Standing off stage, he noticed a man walking over to him, smiling.

'How about a match to celebrate?' the man proposed as he opened his hand to show a collection of old beer-cap chips and tree-bark cards. The two held hands, walked out of the bookshop and floated softly into the park without saying a word. Tony was full of warmth, excitement and nerves with everything being so new. He, nonetheless, was calmed by the change. They arrived at the park, and Carlos headed over to their old oak tree.

'Why don't we sit under this one instead?' Tony proposed.

'Sure, no worries. I'll beat you anyway,' Carlos joked back.

As they walked closer to the tree, Tony put his arm around Carlos and smiled at a single leaf swaying in the wind. He looked at Carlos, and then at the leaf, and said, 'You really are a beautiful tree.'

The Leaf That Never Fell

THE CHEF WHO LOST HIS SALSA

The Chef Who Lost His Salsa

José was a happy, simple man. Cooking was his passion, his wife Monica was his devotion and his Colombian restaurant, La Bamba, was the centre of his world. José originally started as a street vendor, preparing his abuela's famous Milanese con Papas Fritas (crumbed chicken with fried potato chips) for the hungry and curious patrons of Melbourne who waited in mile-long queues.

'Buenos Dias Amigos,' José would sing as he opened his vendor doors and danced into the kitchen to start peeling potatoes. 'Isn't this the perfect day for Colombian food everybody?!'

The guests didn't mind waiting, even for an hour or two. La Bamba's vibe and scent would fill the streets with warmth, like a Colombian family welcoming you into their home.

However, the lines at La Bamba weren't always so lengthy. In fact, when La Bamba first opened, Colombian food was a flavour that had not yet touched the tongues of Melbournians. Yet, José's famous dishes, rich in flavour and spice, soon became the talk of the town. It was not long after this that José's small pop-up eatery grew into a colourful and much-loved restaurant and 'one of Melbourne's most authentic and vibrant experiences', according to a well-acclaimed food critic.

'If I don't see love in your eyes when you take your first bite, Milaneses on me!' José promised his guests, and he was yet to pay for a single dish. José had it all figured out: calming clave sounds to start the evening and catch the exhausted after-work diners, a little more cowbell for the

The Chef Who Lost His Salsa

take away orders, and, then—BAM—crispy, spicy salsa for the crazy rush hour. It was always at this point of the evening that José would come out from the kitchen, whip his hand towel from around his neck and, in front of the guests, bow before his wife Monica, the restaurant manager, as if proposing to the art of salsa itself.

'May I salsa with my amor?' José would request.

'Always, my José,' Monica would respond as she flung herself into her husband's arms.

The two would then salsa around the restaurant, in between tables, sometimes even out the door onto the street and back again in a very lively performance. The guests loved it, applauding and screaming long after José salsaed back into the kitchen to continue service, and Monica snapped back into working on the floor. Throughout their lives in Melbourne, José and Monica tried hard to keep true to their Colombian culture. They had their Colombian restaurant, and, of course, their beloved salsa dancing, which they committed to every Sunday at the Night Cat on Johnston Street.

Each time, without fail, while eagerly waiting in the line to salsa, José would gaze at Monica with romantic eyes and acknowledge 'isn't this the perfect night for salsaing, my Monica?'

'Yes, José, you are so right,' she would respond, as if she had never realised it before.

The pair would Salsa all night long and would regularly

find themselves teaching a crowd how to loosen their ankles. However, Night Cat aside, life in Australia was vastly different than life in Bogota. In Bogota, everyone is family: your neighbour on the bus, the person walking next to you, even your customers would be welcome to stay at your home and regularly come for dinner—no invitations needed! In Bogota, the usual track to work involves dodging soccer matches with the children in almost every street. José had always believed that the most important part of his day was kicking a goal before work. But when José and Monica arrived in Australia, they had to adjust to the Australian way of life. At first, people thought they were always yelling because of their expressive conversational gestures and their passionate pronunciation, and José soon came to realise it was not okay to walk into his neighbour's house without asking to say hello.

As time went on, things didn't stay so romantic for Monica and José nor for La Bamba. In 2016, the queues for La Bamba slowly grew smaller, so much so that there was no need for a waiting list. In no time, José found himself salsaing for only two occupied tables in a restaurant fit to seat twenty-five. Monica started to worry. Then, on one lonely Wednesday evening, as José was salsaing for a small birthday celebration, something terrible happened. His feet suddenly stopped. It was like they were stuck or tremendously confused. They could not remember the next step.

'What is happening?' Monica questioned with fear as she watched José struggle.

'Right foot, left foot, right foot then what?!' José repeated

The Chef Who Lost His Salsa

to himself, trying to help his feet recall what came next. But nothing came. It was then that José realised he had forgotten how to salsa; it was a tragedy! Front-page headlines started appearing in the tabloids:

José of La Bamba Loses His Touch
La Bamba To Go Under
Hey José, Where Did the Love Go?
The Chef Who Lost His Salsa

Customers complained that José's famous Milanese con Papas Fritas tasted bland, ordinary and no different to a parmigiana at the pub. For the first time ever, he was paying for Milaneses—dish after dish. His regulars tried to stay loyal to their 'the usual order' lifestyle; however, they, too, could not deny that something had changed.

José knew he needed to save his restaurant, his salsa and his family, especially because Monica and José were planning on having a child soon, and he knew his finances could in no way support his future niño.

Struggles aside, José still tried to salsa each night. He would plug in his headphones and listen to salsa for hours to prepare for his performance. Monica tried to remind his feet how it was to walk and dance in Colombia, but this, too, did not work. Sadly, José eventually decided to stop salsaing for his guests. After all, performing for an empty restaurant is very exhausting.

One late Monday evening, José sat at table three, secretly smoking his cigar and doing his accounting, when Rico—his long-time staff member since the street-vendor days—

walked up to José with sad, sorry eyes.

'José,' he said calmly, 'you cannot keep paying me for just two tables a night.'

'I know Rico,' sighed José, 'but what am I to do?'

'José, you know we have been friends since we were just little niños, but the customers are right,' Rico explained. 'The flavours have changed, this new taste is not the taste of us in Bogota running around as crazy kids or selling our abuelas' food on the busy streets. This taste is not the taste of birthday fiestas and chopping parsley and chilli. This is not La Bamba. You must find La Bamba again.' Rico placed his hand on José's shoulder to show he felt for José and that he knew José could do what was necessary to save La Bamba.

José put out his cigar, closed his accounts book and walked home with a head full of thoughts. He wished he could run into a soccer match and kick a goal on his way home to lift his mood. He arrived home and opened the door to find a very angry, frustrated Monica pacing around the house as if she had been anticipating José's return for hours. It seemed she had found José's secret cigar box ... and she was furious.

'José! What have I told you about smoking your cigars when I am trying to get pregnant, the smell makes me get sick!' Monica yelled, holding the cigar box in her hand. 'I found these under your bed!'

'Monica,' José snapped, 'I am working so hard at the

The Chef Who Lost His Salsa

restaurant. I'm sorry!'

They both screamed and shouted as loud as their voices would allow. Their fight carried on throughout the house and throughout the long night. Monica eventually slammed her door and ordered José to leave her alone, so José listened and took himself to the kitchen. After all, it was 11pm, and they had forgotten to eat dinner.

José, full of emotion, forcefully pulled open the fridge door, grabbed some chicken fillets he had bought from the market and passionately pounded them with his hands to tenderise the meat. He chopped the parsley so quickly that his chopping looked magical. He buried the chicken in breadcrumbs and tossed it in the hot oil. He unevenly chopped some rustic potatoes found in the bottom drawer and threw them in the oil, too. After the meal cooked and filled the room with its delicious aromas, José served it up and took a well-deserved bite. José's eyes widened. 'It's Bogota! It's La Bamba!' he yelled, as he raced up to his wife to feed her his meal. She grumpily took one bite, and couldn't help but raise her eyebrows.

'It tastes like your abuela's,' she pronounced with joy, 'I can't believe it!' She screamed, and the couple jumped up and down, celebrating, hugging, singing. José whipped his hand-towel from around his neck, bowed before his wife as a request to salsa. Tensions were high as Monica worried that José's feet had still forgotten Colombia, and that it would ruin this beautiful moment. He grabbed her hand, and, as if nothing was ever wrong, they salsaed around the house, around the kitchen table, up onto the couch and down again, even through their apartment corridor all the way to the street.

'My darling, I feel the passion again. That's what was missing,' José exclaimed with relief. It was their passionate fight that had kicked the Colombian spirit back into José. He realised exactly what he needed to do. He was Colombian, a lively, passionate Colombian. The world wouldn't work any other way, and neither would La Bamba. All José needed to do was remember his roots, and the La Bamba queues would follow.

And so La Bamba continued as crazy as it was always destined to be. As time went on, the lines hugged the blocks again, and the guests had a new favourite show: Monica and her first son, Alejandro, performing their sweet mother and son salsa dance after the Milaneses were served (by the way, they were better than ever).

José would come out of the kitchen and join the colourful salsa dance as one big passionate Colombian family living in the wonderful city of Melbourne. Even Rico would join too.

The Chef Who Lost His Salsa

STOP 36

Stop 36

Every day for Clara is much the same. Samsung alarm birds mark her 6am rise. Snooze, of course. Just five minutes. Then another three. Sometimes, if she's feeling extra tired, an extra two. Then, 'Shit, I really have to get up.'

Shower. Cigarette. Go.

The bus stop is close to Clara's house, about a minute's walk, and the bus goes direct to the call centre where she works. Selling university degrees, something helpful. She tells herself she's bettering society. This gets her through. Eight hours of work, scripted gibberish, after-work whisky, Netflix, bed. Clara is pretty sick of it. But isn't everyone?

She often thinks about working at one of those busy cafés that plays fun music, or even the museum where she could just relax. But Clara wonders if, after a year or two, she would get sick of that too. 'Will I ever be happy? Will anyone?'

Clara always seems to make the bus, but today she is really pushing it, running down Errol Street still gargling mouthwash. She makes it and embraces the day, zombie style.

'Morning Veronika,' Clara greets the bus driver. 'Hey Clara ... you look like shit!' replies Veronika, the never-taking-life-too-seriously, great-advice-giving figure in Clara's life.

'Thanks V,' Clara replies sarcastically. She takes her seat,

Stop 36

Stop 36

plugs her earphones in and Stone Roses it up. She rests her head on the window, confident she's resting and certainly not sleeping.

Clara's eyes hatch open just as she realises she is one of those fools who falls asleep and misses their stop. 'Stop 35! I was supposed to get off at 29!'

She inspects the bus and spots only one other person besides Veronika. Feeling like an utter twat, Clara gets up and presses the big red 'next stop' button. They are approaching stop 36 when the bus starts to rumble, rattle and rock, and Veronika suddenly speeds up.

'Veronika! What are you doing?!' Clara shouts, panicking. They are now at 150 kilometres per hour, and Clara is freaking the hell out. 'What's going on? Stop!' Clara's stomach drops as the bus starts to launch off the ground. 'Oh my god! The bus is flying!' Clara yells.

BANG!

'Three cappuccinos and two oat lattes,' a blonde waitress barks at Clara.

New Order is pumping (a café favourite), and Clara is standing at a coffee machine frothing milk. Somehow, someway, Clara is the cool barista chick, making killer coffees. What is happening?

Clara shoots out the orders, making cute little love heart pictures with the milk for the guys on table three. She has no idea what is going on, but, what the hell, she rolls

Stop 36

with it, singing along, making barista jokes, and even pretending to get angry at customer's stupid coffee orders. Truth is, she really doesn't care at all but wants to fully channel the typical attitude of a too-good-for-a-¾ full-oat latte barista. This is fun.

It's now 3pm and the day is near its end for the cool barista chick. Clara can't believe she is finishing at 3.30pm. She packs up the coffee machine, high fives the other café staff and walks to the bus stop.

The bus arrives ... It's Veronika! 'So Clara, how was your day?' questions Veronika with a cheeky grin that indicates she already knows it was interesting.

'Yeah V, it was good! But what the hell happened?' asks Clara, intrigued.

'Well, Clara, you missed your stop and wound up at stop 36. Stop 36 is where people go when they are fed up with their boring jobs, and they get to exchange jobs with another passenger for a day. But it's a secret. So don't say a word. The other passenger on the bus, Olivia, went to work for you today, and you handled her barista job.'

Olivia gets on the bus. 'Hey, Clara, cool job!' she says.

'Hey, Olivia, you too! Thanks for that,' replies Clara, grinning. Veronika closes the doors and drives them both home as usual. Clara skips down Errol Street, belting out New Order, excited for her next stop 36 adventure.

Stop 36

PUNK IS NOT DEAD

'Bing bing bing BING!' The ascending notes of the school bell always elicit drag in Sidney. 'Another day with these fools,' Sidney thinks on this very regular Tuesday morning. Sidney is a keep-to-himself type of student. It's not like he's shy; he just feels misunderstood. Damien and Jade are his parents. I guess you could describe them as individuals. Do-it-yourself type thinkers with an open-minded parenting style. Really, they're just straight-out punks. Hence their son's name, Sidney, after Sidney Vicious from the Sex Pistols.

And so it was that Sidney grew up to be a punk, too. He learnt guitar notes before his alphabet and has been spraying his hair crazy colours for as long as he can remember. However, being a punk in a world full of normalcy can be undeniably lonely. People just don't understand.

It's time for class, and as Sidney scuffs his leather boots along the hallway, he wonders why it is that punks have been forgotten. 'Punks have done so much for this world, and I wish people could just understand,' Sidney wishes. He reaches his classroom: room H18.

'Good Morning Sidney,' greets Mr Hamilton. 'I hope you are excited for work experience week. Have you got everything organised?' he questions faithfully.

'Sure, Mr Hamilton, I can't wait,' lies Sidney. Truth be told, Sidney has nothing at all. Nothing has called to him.

'Excuse me, Sidney,' interrupts a sweet classmate. 'I'm working at a makeup store for work experience, and was wondering if you could help me with Goth makeup?' she

Punk Is Not Dead

asks politely.

'I'm sorry,' Sidney sighs. 'I'm not a Goth.'

But this isn't the first time Sidney has been mistaken for something other than a punk. He often gets confused for a metalhead, too, and sometimes, on the odd occasion, an emo. It's no wonder Sidney feels misunderstood.

A short tram ride to Flinders Street Station is Sidney's track home. Packed tram, exhausted workers, nothing unusual or intriguing to him. But today, Sidney notices something different.

'And here comes the number 5 tram everybody, all aboard,' announces a short, friendly man. He has a microphone, and it seems his profession is to MC the tram schedule.

'Nice shoes,' the man says, complimenting a passenger on his way home from work.

He is hilarious, and, suddenly, Sidney has a thought. 'I'm going to be a tram MC for work experience and educate the world on punks! We will be heard!' Sidney proclaims.

It was now work experience week, and Sidney has built up much anticipation for his, as he calls it, 'Punk Education Class'. He wears a black and white suit, as requested, but rocks a tartan red tie to mark his punk ethnicity. A short introduction at the Flinders Street Station office teaches Sidney that, as well as introducing the trams and safety rules, he must also be engaging, entertaining and, according to the short, friendly man: 'a fun guy!'

Punk Is Not Dead

'I think I can do that,' replies Sidney with a suggestive grin.

'Great. Here is your microphone,' replies the man with great belief and trust in Sidney.

The number 16 tram approaches the sea of commuters eager to get down St Kilda Road. Sidney clears his throat. 'Aaaaaaaand here comes the number 16 tram everybody. Watch your step passengers ... The number 16 tram everybody ... hmm 16, that's the age when I first started rebelling and speaking up,' announces Sidney.

'How about you, sir?' Sidney asks, questioning an older fellow.

'Shut up and leave me alone!' the older fellow snaps back.

'Yes, that's right. Question authority! Punks influenced the rebel movement, and we sure are proud of you, sir,' teaches Sidney.

The man does not respond and only raises an eyebrow.

'And now the number 8, number 8 everybody number 8 ...' Sidney declares.

He then notices a small man struggling to board the tram with a huge cello. Sidney offers to help and asks the cello man, 'Excuse me fellow musician, are you in a band?'

'Oh no. I would love to be, but we are not quite there yet,' the cello man replies.

Punk Is Not Dead

'Well, do you know punks were the ones who taught us, you don't need to be signed to show off your talent. All the best, sir,' says Sidney.

'Oh, thank you!' the cello man responds.

'Welcome to the floor. The number 6 tram, three minutes late, but it's all good everyone: punks accept individuals,' Sidney jokes. 'The number 6 tram everybody ... number 6 ... do you know this suit I'm wearing only cost $6? That's right, I made it myself. Punks introduced the DIY trend years ago,' Sidney educates.

'Great job. It looks great,' a wide-smiled blonde woman exclaims, complimenting Sidney. 'I made my dress, too,' she shouts as she boards the tram.

Sidney is filled with a sense of accomplishment, joy and, most apparently, pride.

He continues to MC the transport schedule throughout the day, teaching society all types of punk facts. He even speaks to a young art student, suggesting that he create a collage for his next piece. 'Do you know punks invented the collage, too?' he teaches the art student.

Finally, Sidney's day comes to an end, and just as he begins his route home, he spots the sweet girl from his class, also on her way home from work experience.

'Hi Sidney. I heard you while I was boarding my tram this morning, and then learnt all about punk makeup—particularly bold and fierce eyes.'

'Wow that's fantastic!' Sidney replies.

'See you tomorrow,' the sweet girl hollers just before she runs to catch her tram.

Sidney arrives home and is, for once, excited for school tomorrow—which is only a dinner and a sleep away. He rests his head and sleeps with a smile on his face. Feeling well-accomplished, well-experienced, well-worked and, most of all, finally well-understood.

Punk Is Not Dead

LOLITA'S CHATTY CASA

Lolita grew up in buzzing London town where the crowds, at times, carry you, and the sun offers cherished moments of grace. She loves what her city offers: how she can hear her neighbours' tea parties through the wall, the never-ending array of art exhibitions that can be found and lost, and how, on any one day, she can stumble across a new part of the city she has never, in her twenty-eight years of life, known before. That's why, every morning, she goes on an adventure—all day long.

A typical day for Lolita involves running through parks, jumping on buses, discovering new underpasses, and—her favourite activity of all—finding abandoned buildings where she can write until the sun goes down. Then, just before the sky turns a true pitch black, she runs through the last glimmer of daylight and treks home. Sometimes, she gets lost on her way back, but that doesn't bother Lolita; it simply excites her. She often wonders what she would do in a big empty house anyway, which is the exact thought that, more often than not, keeps her out all night long.

When she arrives home, she always heads straight to her bathroom, has a shower and moisturises her entire body before surrendering to the day that was. However, on the nights she makes it home, a BANG often wakes her: the sound of a lightbulb, door knob or ornament smashing completely to the floor. It is all very strange, but Lolita has been dealing with this issue for so long that, without fuss, she gets up and collects the broken objects, placing them next to her bed to mend the following day. Sometimes, she even does this in her sleep, waking the next morning, shocked at what has broken, shouting something like, 'Not Aunt Margie's cigarette box!' Lolita has tried everything to fix the strange breakages, but, sadly, nothing has worked, and she has grown to accept that they are here to stay.

On this particular Thursday morning, Lolita is busy gluing a sculpture of the earth back together when an unusual announcement comes on the radio.

'ATTENTION ALL LONDONERS: The animals from the local zoo have broken out of their enclosures and are rummaging through the streets, attacking anyone they see. Experts say they've been in confined and unnatural spaces for too long, and they've simply gone insane. Because of the dangers on our streets, everyone is to stay indoors until further notice.'

Lolita drops her tea mug, and it smashes into a million pieces. 'Oh no,' she shouts. 'Not only am I stuck inside, but I have another breakage to fix. What am I going to do? I don't have enough moisturiser left to lather myself all day; my world is ending!'

After hours of trolling the news and sinking deeper and deeper into frightening headlines—50,000 LION ATTACKS PREDICTED ON THOSE WHO SNEAK OUT FOR ICE CREAM and ZEAL OF ZEBRAS PETITION OUTSIDE DOWNING STREET—Lolita decides this is no way to deal with a crisis and that she really should do something productive. 'I know!' she cries, 'I'm going to fix every broken object in my home!' And so, Lolita makes a list of everything that needs fixing and heads to bed feeling enthused.

Lolita's Chatty Casa

Lolita slowly opens her eyes the next morning and realises she has slept through her usual 8am alarm. Normally, she leaves the house at 9am, but it's 10am, an out-of-the-ordinary scenario. Everything feels different today. Lolita walks downstairs in her underwear to make a coffee, but, to her complete shock, she hears conversations going on in the kitchen like there's a booming stock on Wall Street: voices leap over each other amidst bursts of laughter and clapping.

'What are these voices?' Lolita frightfully asks herself as she stands still in her doorway. 'Am I being robbed?' she begins to wonder before quickly realising that robbers wouldn't be sitting in the kitchen having what sounds like a party. 'Then what's going on?' Lolita whispers, and remains confused.

After a few minutes of trying to figure out who's in her kitchen, Lolita collects all of the courage she has in her body, and flings open the door—but the chattering immediately stops, and the room is empty. How could this be? Lolita creeps into her kitchen, toes touching the tiles one by one, and suspiciously clicks down the kettle—but the kettle starts screaming at her.

'Why are you home and using me? I have plans with my partner,' the kettle pronounces.

'OH MY GOSH,' Lolita screams as she jumps back.

'Yes, my wife and I are about to get real hot together,' says the toaster, and Lolita snaps her attention to him. 'You

barely use us anyway,' the toaster goes on.
'I'm sorry what did you say?!' Lolita asks, full of fear, as the toaster and the kettle start heating up.

Lolita creeps out of the kitchen, confused, but decides to give them some privacy. Still trying to figure out what's going on, Lolita decides to head upstairs and start fixing the lightbulb, which regularly bursts in her sitting room. She climbs up the ladder and starts to unscrew the bulb, but then it starts crying.

'There's no use in fixing me. I've been dealing with your jumping for years, and it's taken its toll. I'm officially unfixable.'

Lolita feels deeply sad and responds, 'I'm sorry ... umm ... I'm so sorry ... I didn't know ...' and slowly steps down the ladder almost in tears with guilt. 'I'm sorry Lightbulb. I will stop jumping,' Lolita promises, and she closes the door.

It's been a strange morning for Lolita, but she decides to continue on with her plan to mend her home. She heads to her bedroom, to the broken vase that smashed off her mantlepiece last week, and tries to figure out how the pieces will fit back together. She pulls the glue from her pocket when the pieces start yelling.

'I'LL BREAK AGAIN, I'LL BREAK A THOUSAND TIMES OVER IF I HAVE TO LOOK AT THAT CHEATING LAMP FOR ANOTHER SECOND.'

'The cheating what?!' Lolita responds, looking at the

lamp, who turns around one-hundred and eighty degrees to avoid responsibility.

Lolita decides to move to another room to try her luck when she hears another announcement on the radio downstairs in her chatty kitchen. She walks downstairs, hoping the toaster and kettle have finished their business, and knocks on the door.

'Yes?' the toaster responds. 'We have our choir group in ten minutes and the spoons are already warming up.'

Lolita looks at the spoons as they clink themselves together in a catchy rhythm. 'I'll be quick,' she says as she enters and turns on the radio.

'ATTENTION ALL LONDONERS: there was an attempt today to move the animals to a man-made jungle, but, unfortunately, the animals have rebelled. Experts say it's not what the animals want, and they are more angry than before. Because of this, officials ask that all residents stay inside and keep their windows closed. Please stay tuned for more news.'

The whole house begins to boo and yell, and the pot plants start spinning in anger shouting, 'This is a disaster! Now she will be home all the time and we can't do our regular activities!'

Lolita is really offended and feels like a stranger in her house. 'I'm sorry you feel this way, but you can do what you like,' she insists and walks through the house so every object can hear her.

Lolita's Chatty Casa

'No, we cannot. You have neglected us for years, and we've created our own world that can't exist with you here,' the pillows say.

Lolita doesn't know what to say, or which room to go to next, so she says nothing at all and sits on the floor, while her objects huff and puff around her. Lolita feels tremendous guilt and starts to understand why her objects are like this; that each item has its own story, emotions and needs, just like humans and just like the animals at the zoo. If she wants her house to be fixed, she needs to fix all of the conflict first, but this could take months, as it's been years since she has spent quality time at home. But she is willing to take on the mission.

'I will fix this house. I promise,' Lolita proclaims. 'I want to get to know each and every one of you,' she continues, as the objects say nothing at all. 'Please think tonight about what you want to share with me tomorrow, what you need to make you happy, and I'm here to listen for as long as it takes,' Lolita announces. The objects still say nothing and continue amongst themselves. 'Okay, well, goodnight home,' Lolita shares, as she climbs the stairs and heads to bed.

The next day, Lolita gets up early, ready to fix her home. She starts by moving some objects. 'Is this a better spot for you?' she asks the cabinet.

'Yes, actually, I have never liked being in a corner,' he responds, and he thanks Lolita.

'That one was easy,' Lolita declares to herself, feeling more positive. She then moves onto the vase and the lamp and sits them opposite each other in a couples therapy-type situation.

'Now, Vase, I know you are in pieces over this break-up, literally, but I think it would be good if you told Lamp exactly how you feel,' suggests Lolita.

'I'm here to listen,' says Lamp.

'Well, I told you for months that Torso was flirting with you, and you called me crazy, but then you ended up cheating on me with her, I mean, do you understand my frustration?' the vase pieces say.

'I'm so sorry Vase—I don't even like Torso. I regret everything and I love you,' Lamp says while bursting into tears.

'It's too late, Lamp, but thank you for your apology. I would still like to be moved Lolita,' insists Vase.

'Absolutely Vase. I will mend you, and you will have a fresh start,' Lolita responds.

Lamp begins to cry. 'I will think about you every day,' he weeps.

'And you should,' agrees Lolita, 'but this is your fresh start, too.'

Lolita mends the vase and places her downstairs, ordering some fresh flowers so she feels great about her new life.

Lolita is really enjoying the experience of getting to know her home. And so, Lolita spends the next few months listening to her objects and understanding their needs, a simple strategy that the objects respond exceptionally well to. If the spoon choir wants steel drums for its band, she makes them. If the lightbulb wants to be completely rewired, she teaches herself how to do it.

While getting to know her home, she learns of the relationship between her two art pieces, who have had feelings for each other since they were hung on the same wall ten years ago. She separated them during a spring clean, and they've been thinking of each other ever since. The Joan Miró painting shares with Lolita that he wants to marry the Botero sculpture upstairs; he is sick of waiting, and Lolita wants to make this happen.

'So, how do you want to propose, Painting? Lolita asks.

'Well, I was thinking you could reframe me so I look better than ever, and then you could take me upstairs and dim the lights for my proposal. Could you do that?' asks Painting.

'Of course!' she responds.

'Well, I'm ready to slip into a new frame when you are.

'Okay, I better get straight to it.'

'And if she says yes, the wedding will be a great chance for the house to all be together,' adds Painting.

On the day of the proposal, Lolita spends the entire morning cleaning the house. The painting is sitting nervously on the wall, in the fantastic new frame that Lolita built for him. The house is sparkling, and Lolita is chatting to all of the objects about what is going on in their lives when she realises she has completely lost track of time. She notices that it is already dark outside, so she runs to the painting.

'Painting, it's time!' she bursts out, grabbing and rushing him upstairs to right outside the room where Sculpture lives. Lolita dims the lights, which work so smoothly now that Lightbulb is rewired. They enter the room.

'Hello Sculpture,' greets Painting.

'Oh my gosh! Painting! Oh, I ... I can't believe it! You look great,' Sculpture says, flustered.

'Lolita has been spending time around the house, giving the objects what they want,' begins Painting, 'and, well, what would make me happy would be if we could be together, in the same room, forever ... so ... will you marry me?' Painting proposes as Lolita gets down on one knee, holding him.

'Oh my gosh, oh my gosh, oh my gosh!' replies Sculpture. 'YES!'

Lolita jumps up and twirls the painting around as the whole house applauds, whistles and screams. 'Now,' shouts Lolita, 'let's plan a party!'

It's the day of the party, and the objects are so pleased to see one another and can't stop chatting while the new spring sun beams through the windows. Lamp has become a marriage officiant on his mission to become a better lamp, finding great joy in binding the love between objects.

'You are now husband and wife,' he announces, as Painting and Sculpture share a kiss and everyone yells and screams.

Lolita stands at the back of the room grinning, looking at all of her objects and feeling happy in her chatty home. She walks to the kitchen and turns on the radio as another breaking news announcement commences.

'ATTENTION ALL LONDONERS: The decision has been made to send the animals back to their native homes, as experts say this is what they truly want. The city is now safe. Open your shops, hug your family and enjoy the outdoors.'

Lolita rushes to the door and opens it as a chill runs up and down her body thinking of the animals experiencing the exact same feelings. The world is free again.

The next day, Lolita gets up to adventure: she greets every object in her house and stays home all morning, catching up with the objects before going out in the afternoon. She talks to Painting and Sculpture to find they are still giggly newlyweds—this makes her happy.

Lolita finds a new abandoned area that day, the zoo that

has closed down for good, and writes all about what she has learnt: that choosing absence will only end in cheating lamps and crying lightbulbs.

Lolita's Chatty Casa

Thanks for reading.